The Orchard Book of
NURSERY RHYMES
FOR YOUR BABY

For Matthew, Luca, Tommy and Rosa,
with love – P.D.

ORCHARD BOOKS
Carmelite House
50 Victoria Embankment
London EC4Y 0DZ

First published in 2010 by Orchard Books

A CIP catalogue record for this book is available from the
British Library.

ISBN 978 1 40830 458 7

10 9 8 7
Printed in Malaysia

Orchard Books
An imprint of Hachette Children's Group
Part of The Watts Publishing Group Limited
An Hachette UK Company
www.hachette.co.uk

NURSERY RHYMES
FOR YOUR BABY

Illustrated by Penny Dann

Foreword by Mary Ann Hoberman

ORCHARD

Contents

Sharing Nursery Rhymes with Your Baby

One of the treasures of the English language is its store of songs and verses that go by the collective name of nursery rhymes. Handed down through the generations from parent to child, they are the infant's first introduction to poetry and to the powers and pleasures of language. Lucky the young baby who is bounced along to the rhythm of 'Diddle, Diddle, Dumpling' or claps hands to the beat of 'Pat-a-Cake'.

In passing on these rhymes, you are bestowing a precious heritage. In today's world, with so many of our connections to our common past disappearing, there is a deep satisfaction in keeping this tradition alive, in knowing that you and your child are the newest links in a chain that goes back for centuries.

Out of the hundreds of nursery rhymes now known, this book includes a generous sampling. For native English speakers, many verses will probably be familiar, although they may recall them in slightly different forms. For those whose first language is not English, some of the rhymes may call up counterparts in their own languages. One of the pleasures of a collection like this is the memory jog it provides, not only for rhymes included here but for others, not here but now suddenly called to mind.

These days, teachers stress the importance of nursery rhymes in laying the groundwork for reading and the acquisition of language skills. But I would rather talk about the joys these rhymes provide right now, the way their catchy rhymes and rhythms invite both romping and snuggling, giggles and cuddles.

For, above all else, they are fun! Fun for the adult, fun for the child! Fun to say, fun to chant, fun to sing! Always available, free for the taking, they offer the perfect soundtrack for most of childhood's experiences. Heard early, learned by heart, they convey both the sense and the nonsense of words, the puns and the playfulness inherent in language.

The wonderful thing about these rhymes is that once learned they are never entirely forgotten. Throughout one's life they remain encoded in memory, keeping us connected to the feelings and sensations of our earliest years. And, when the time comes, ready to be passed on with joy to a new generation.

Mary Ann Hoberman

This Little Piggy

Old Macdonald Had a Farm

Old Macdonald had a farm,
E-I-E-I-O!
And on that farm he had some ducks,
E-I-E-I-O!
With a quack quack here,
And a quack quack there,
Here a quack, there a quack,
Everywhere a quack quack,
Old Macdonald had a farm,
E-I-E-I-O!

Old Macdonald had a farm,
E-I-E-I-O!
And on that farm he had some cows,
E-I-E-I-O!
With a moo moo here,
And a moo moo there,
Here a moo, there a moo,
Everywhere a moo moo,
Old Macdonald had a farm,
E-I-E-I-O!

Old Macdonald had a farm,
E-I-E-I-O!
And on that farm he had some pigs,
E-I-E-I-O!
With an oink oink here,
And an oink oink there,
Here an oink, there an oink,
Everywhere an oink oink,
Old Macdonald had a farm,
E-I-E-I-O!

Quack!

Oink!

Old Macdonald had a farm
E-I-E-I-O!
And on that farm he had some sheep,
E-I-E-I-O!
With a baa baa here,
And a baa baa there,
Here a baa, there a baa,
Everywhere a baa baa,
Old Macdonald had a farm,
E-I-E-I-O!

Baa!

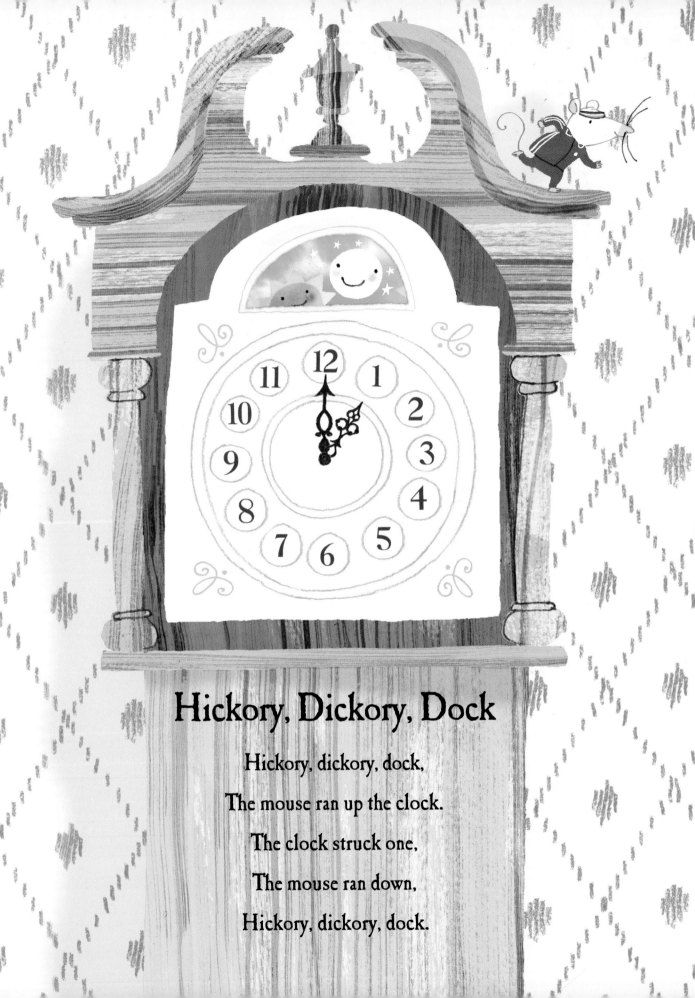

Hickory, Dickory, Dock

Hickory, dickory, dock,

The mouse ran up the clock.

The clock struck one,

The mouse ran down,

Hickory, dickory, dock.

Baa, Baa, Black Sheep

Baa, baa, black sheep,

Have you any wool?

Yes, sir, yes, sir,

Three bags full;

One for the master,

And one for the dame,

And one for the little boy

Who lives down the lane.

Little Miss Muffet

Little Miss Muffet

Sat on a tuffet,

Eating her curds and whey;

Along came a spider,

Who sat down beside her

And frightened Miss Muffet away.

Pussycat, Pussycat

Pussycat, pussycat, where have you been?

I've been to London to visit the queen.

Pussycat, pussycat, what did you there?

I frightened a little mouse under her chair.

Three Blind Mice

Three blind mice, three blind mice,

See how they run! See how they run!

They all ran after the farmer's wife,

Who cut off their tails with a carving knife,

Did you ever see such a thing in your life,

As three blind mice?

Little Bo Peep

Little Bo Peep has lost her sheep,

And doesn't know where to find them;

Leave them alone, and they'll come home,

Wagging their tails behind them.

17

Three Little Kittens

Three little kittens, they lost their mittens,

And they began to cry,

Oh, Mother dear, we sadly fear

Our mittens we have lost.

What! Lost your mittens,

You naughty kittens!

Then you shall have no pie.

Meow, meow, meow.

No, you shall have no pie.

The three little kittens, they found their mittens,

And they began to cry,

Oh, Mother dear, see here, see here,

Our mittens we have found.

Put on your mittens,

You silly kittens,

And you shall have some pie.

Purr, purr, purr,

Oh, let us have some pie.

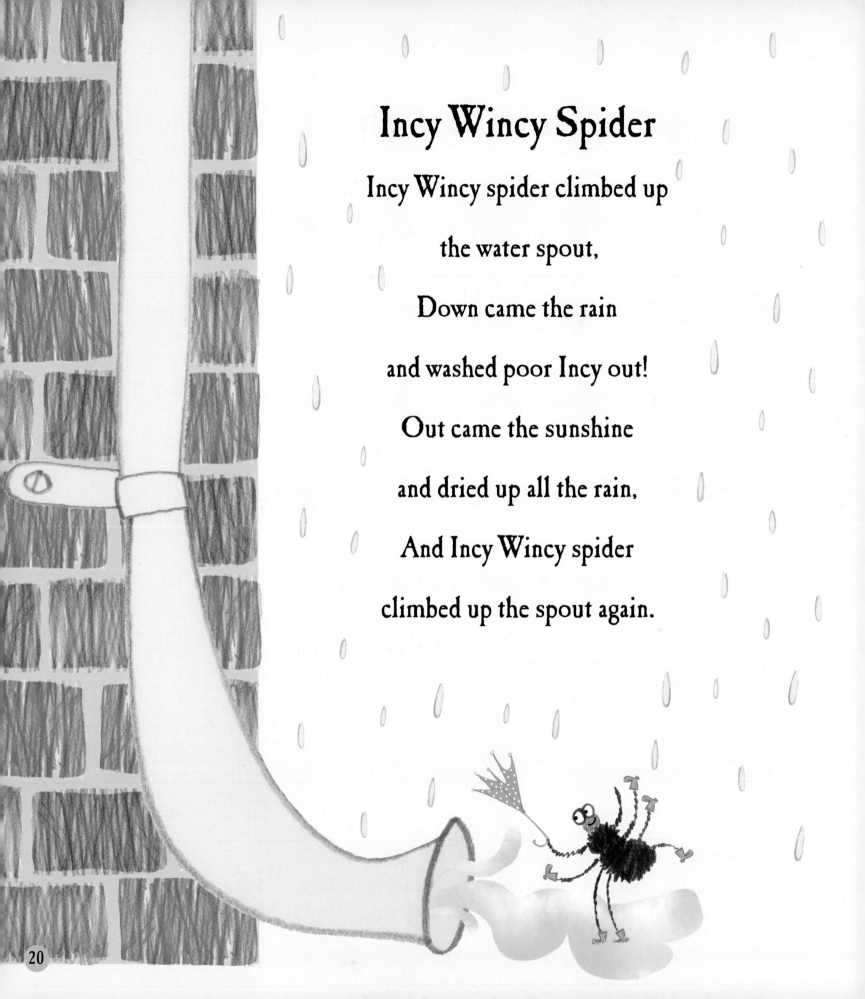

Incy Wincy Spider

Incy Wincy spider climbed up

the water spout,

Down came the rain

and washed poor Incy out!

Out came the sunshine

and dried up all the rain,

And Incy Wincy spider

climbed up the spout again.

This Little Piggy

This little piggy went to market,

This little piggy stayed at home,

This little piggy had roast beef,

This little piggy had none,

And this little piggy cried,

Wee, wee,

wee, wee!

all the way home.

Hey Diddle, Diddle

Hey diddle, diddle,

The cat and the fiddle,

The cow jumped over the moon;

The little dog laughed

To see such sport,

And the dish ran away with the spoon.

My Black Hen

Hickety, pickety, my black hen,

She lays eggs for gentlemen;

Sometimes nine and sometimes ten,

Hickety, pickety, my black hen.

Cock-a-Doodle-Doo!

Cock-a-doodle-doo!

My dame has lost her shoe,

My master's lost his fiddling stick,

And doesn't know what to do.

Mary Had a Little Lamb

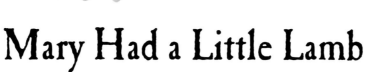

Mary had a little lamb,

Its fleece was white as snow;

And everywhere that Mary went

The lamb was sure to go.

All the King's Men

Sing a Song of Sixpence

Sing a song of sixpence,

a pocket full of rye;

Four and twenty blackbirds,

baked in a pie;

When the pie was opened,

the birds began to sing;

Wasn't that a dainty dish,

to set before the king?

The king was in his counting-house,

counting out his money;

The queen was in the parlour,

eating bread and honey.

The maid was in the garden,

hanging out the clothes,

When down came a blackbird

and pecked off her nose.

The Grand Old Duke of York

Oh, the grand old Duke of York,

He had ten thousand men;

He marched them up to the top of the hill,

And he marched them down again.

And when they were up, they were up,

And when they were down, they were down,

And when they were only halfway up,

They were neither up nor down.

Old King Cole

Old King Cole
Was a merry old soul,
And a merry old soul was he;
He called for his pipe, and he called for his bowl,
And he called for his fiddlers three.

Every fiddler he had a fiddle,
And a very fine fiddle had he;
Oh, there's none so rare
As can compare
With King Cole and his fiddlers three.

Humpty Dumpty

Humpty Dumpty sat on a wall,

Humpty Dumpty

had

a

great

fall;

All the king's horses and all the king's men

Couldn't put Humpty together again.

There was a Crooked Man

There was a crooked man,

And he walked a crooked mile,

He found a crooked sixpence

Against a crooked stile;

He bought a crooked cat,

Which caught a crooked mouse,

And they all lived together

In a little crooked house.

Doctor Foster

Doctor Foster went to Gloucester

In a shower of rain;

He stepped in a puddle,

Right up to his middle,

And never went there again!

The Queen of Hearts

The Queen of Hearts
She made some tarts,
All on a summer's day;
The Knave of Hearts
He stole those tarts,
And took them clean away.

The King of Hearts
Called for the tarts,
And beat the Knave full sore;
The Knave of Hearts
Brought back the tarts,
And vowed he'd steal no more.

There Was an Old Woman

There was an old woman who lived in a shoe,

She had so many children she didn't know what to do,

She gave them some broth without any bread;

She hugged them and kissed them and put them to bed.

Lavender's Blue

Lavender's blue, dilly dilly,
Lavender's green;
When I am king, dilly dilly,
You shall be queen.

Who told you so, dilly dilly,
Who told you so?
'Twas my own heart, dilly dilly,
That told me so.

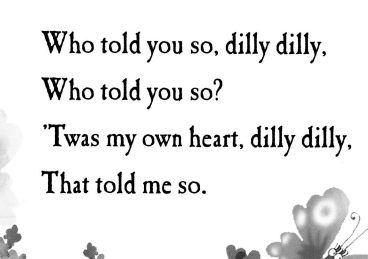

Call up your friends, dilly dilly,
Set them to work,
Some to the plough, dilly dilly,
Some to the fork.

Some to make hay, dilly dilly,
Some to thresh corn,
Whilst you and I, dilly dilly,
Keep ourselves warm.

Girls and Boys

Monday's Child

Monday's child is fair of face,

Tuesday's child is full of grace,

Wednesday's child is full of woe,

Thursday's child has far to go,

Friday's child is loving and giving,

Saturday's child works hard for a living,

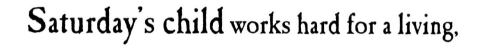

And the child that is born
on the **Sabbath Day**
Is bonny and blithe, and good and gay.

What Are Little Boys Made of?

What are little boys made of?

Frogs and snails, and puppy dogs' tails,

That's what little boys are made of!

What are little girls made of?

Sugar and spice and all things nice,

That's what little girls are made of!

There Was a Little Girl

There was a little girl who had a little curl

Right in the middle of her forehead;

When she was good, she was very, very good,

But when she was bad, she was horrid.

Georgie Porgie

Georgie Porgie, pudding and pie,

Kissed the girls and made them cry;

When the boys came out to play,

Georgie Porgie ran away.

Jack and Jill

Jack and Jill went up the hill,

To fetch a pail of water;

Jack fell down, and broke his crown,

And Jill came tumbling after.

Up Jack got, and home did trot,

As fast as he could caper;

He went to bed to mend his head

With vinegar and brown paper.

Mary, Mary, Quite Contrary

Mary, Mary, quite contrary,

How does your garden grow?

With silver bells and cockle shells,

And pretty maids all in a row.

Lucy Locket

Lucy Locket lost her pocket,

Kitty Fisher found it;

Not a penny was there in it,

Only ribbon round it.

Diddle, Diddle, Dumpling

Diddle, diddle, dumpling, my son John,

Went to bed with his trousers on;

One shoe off and one shoe on,

Diddle, diddle, dumpling, my son John.

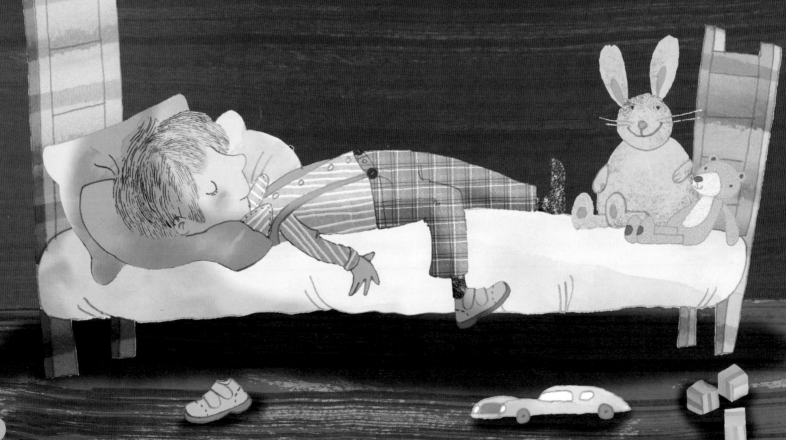

Tom, the Piper's Son

Tom, Tom, the piper's son,

Stole a pig and away did run;

The pig was eat,

And Tom was beat,

And Tom went howling down the street.

One, Two, Three, Four, Five

Five Little Ducks

Five little ducks went swimming one day,

Over the hills and far away.

Mother duck said, "Quack, quack, quack, quack."

But only four little ducks came back.

Four little ducks went swimming one day,

Over the hills and far away.

Mother duck said, "Quack, quack, quack, quack."

But only three little ducks came back.

Three little ducks went swimming one day,

Over the hills and far away.

Mother duck said, "Quack, quack, quack, quack."

But only two little ducks came back.

Two little ducks went swimming one day,

Over the hills and far away.

Mother duck said, "Quack, quack, quack, quack."

But only one little duck came back.

One little duck went swimming one day,

Over the hills and far away.

Mother duck said, "Quack, quack, quack, quack."

And all five little ducks came back.

One, Two, Buckle My Shoe

One, two,
Buckle my shoe;
Three, four, Knock at the door;
Five, six, Pick up sticks;
Seven, eight,
Lay them straight;
Nine, ten,
A big fat hen;

Eleven, twelve, Dig and delve;
Thirteen, fourteen,
Maids a-courting;
Fifteen, sixteen,
Maids in the kitchen;
Seventeen, eighteen,
Maids a-waiting;
Nineteen, twenty,
My plate's empty.

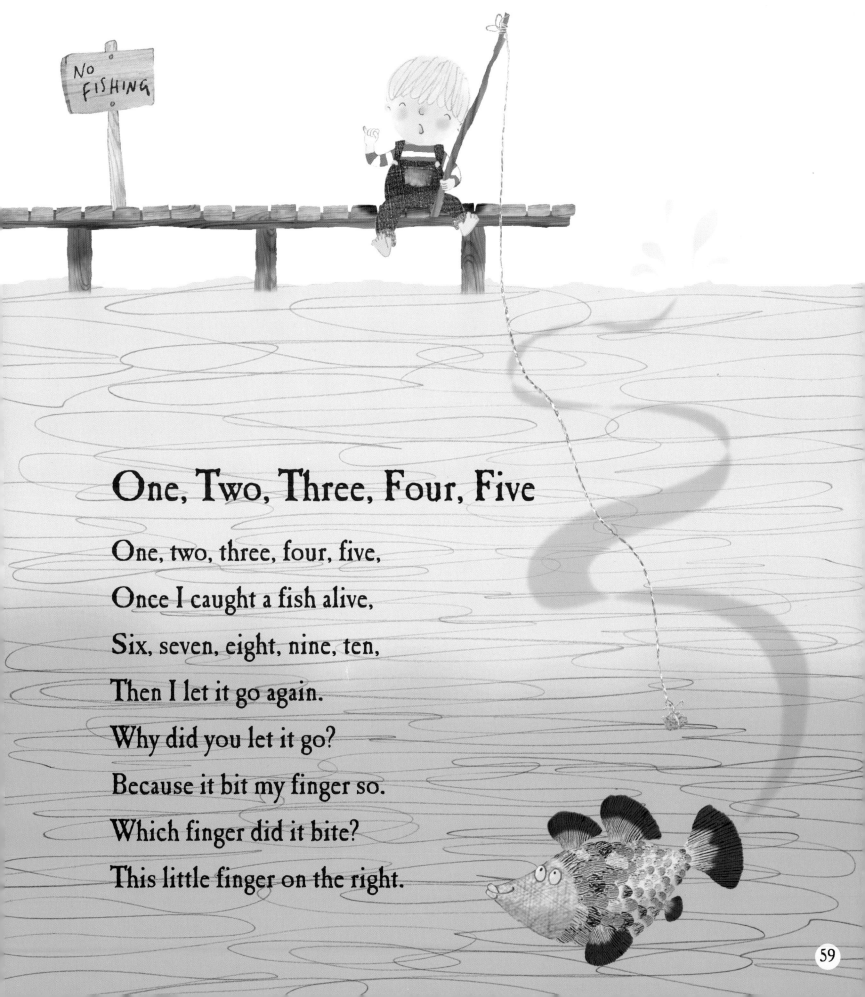

One, Two, Three, Four, Five

One, two, three, four, five,

Once I caught a fish alive,

Six, seven, eight, nine, ten,

Then I let it go again.

Why did you let it go?

Because it bit my finger so.

Which finger did it bite?

This little finger on the right.

Three Little Speckled Frogs

Three little speckled frogs

Sat on a speckled log

Eating the most delicious bugs – yum yum!

One jumped into the pool,

Where it was nice and cool,

Then there were two green speckled frogs – glub glub!

Two little speckled frogs

Sat on a speckled log

Eating the most delicious bugs – yum yum!

One jumped into the pool,

Where it was nice and cool,

Then there was one green speckled frog – glub glub!

One little speckled frog

Sat on a speckled log

Eating the most delicious bugs – yum yum!

She jumped into the pool,

Where it was nice and cool,

Then there were no green speckled frogs – glub glub!

One Potato, Two Potato

One potato, two potato,

Three potato, four,

Five potato, six potato,

Seven potato, more!

more!

Work, Rest and Play

Row, Row, Row Your Boat

Row,

row,

row

your boat,

Gently down

the stream.

Merrily,

   merrily,

      merrily,

         merrily;

Life is but

a dream.

Ring-a-Ring o' Roses

Ring-a-ring o' roses,

A pocket full of posies,

A-tishoo! A-tishoo!

We all fall down.

Seesaw, Margery Daw

Seesaw, Margery Daw,

Johnny shall have a new master;

He shall have but a penny a day,

Because he can't work any faster.

Pop Goes the Weasel

Half a pound of tuppenny rice,
Half a pound of treacle,
That's the way the money goes,
Pop goes the weasel!

All around the carpenter's bench,
The monkey chased the weasel,
That's the way the money goes,
Pop goes the weasel!

Round and Round the Garden

Round and round the garden
Like a teddy bear;
One step, two step,
Tickle you under there!

London Bridge is Falling Down

London Bridge is falling down,

Falling down, falling down,

London Bridge is falling down,

My fair lady.

To Market, To Market

To market, to market,
To buy a fat pig,

Home again, home again,
Jiggety-jig.

To market, to market,
To buy a fat hog,

Home again, home again,
Jiggety-jog.

To market, to market,
To buy a plum bun,

Home again, home again,
Market is done.

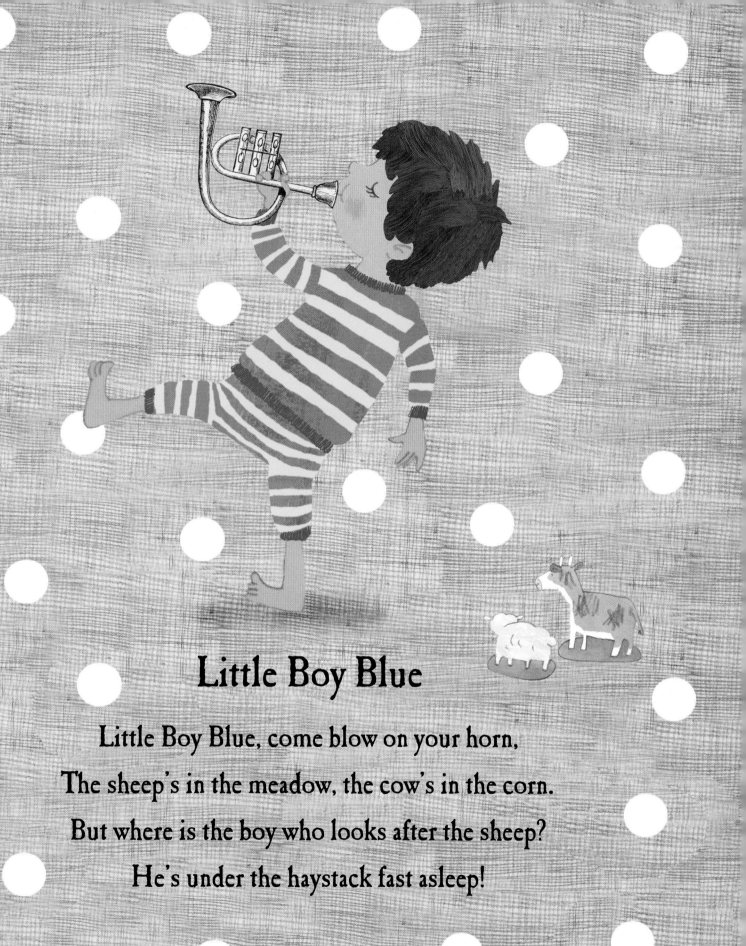

Little Boy Blue

Little Boy Blue, come blow on your horn,

The sheep's in the meadow, the cow's in the corn.

But where is the boy who looks after the sheep?

He's under the haystack fast asleep!

Time for Tea

Polly Put the Kettle On

Polly put the kettle on,
Polly put the kettle on,
Polly put the kettle on,
We'll all have tea.

Sukey take it off again,
Sukey take it off again,
Sukey take it off again,
They've all gone away.

Pat-a-Cake

Pat-a-cake, pat-a-cake, baker's man,

Bake me a cake as fast as you can;

Pat it and prick it and mark it with B,

And put it in the oven for Baby and me.

Little Jack Horner

Little Jack Horner
Sat in the corner,
Eating a Christmas pie;
He put in his thumb,
And pulled out a plum,
And said, What a good boy am I!

Pease Porridge Hot

Pease porridge hot,

Pease porridge cold,

Pease porridge in the pot

Nine days old.

Some like it hot,

Some like it cold,

Some like it in the pot

Nine days old.

Tommy Tucker

Little Tommy Tucker

Sings for his supper:

What shall we give him?

White bread and butter.

How shall he cut it

Without a knife?

How will he be married

Without a wife?

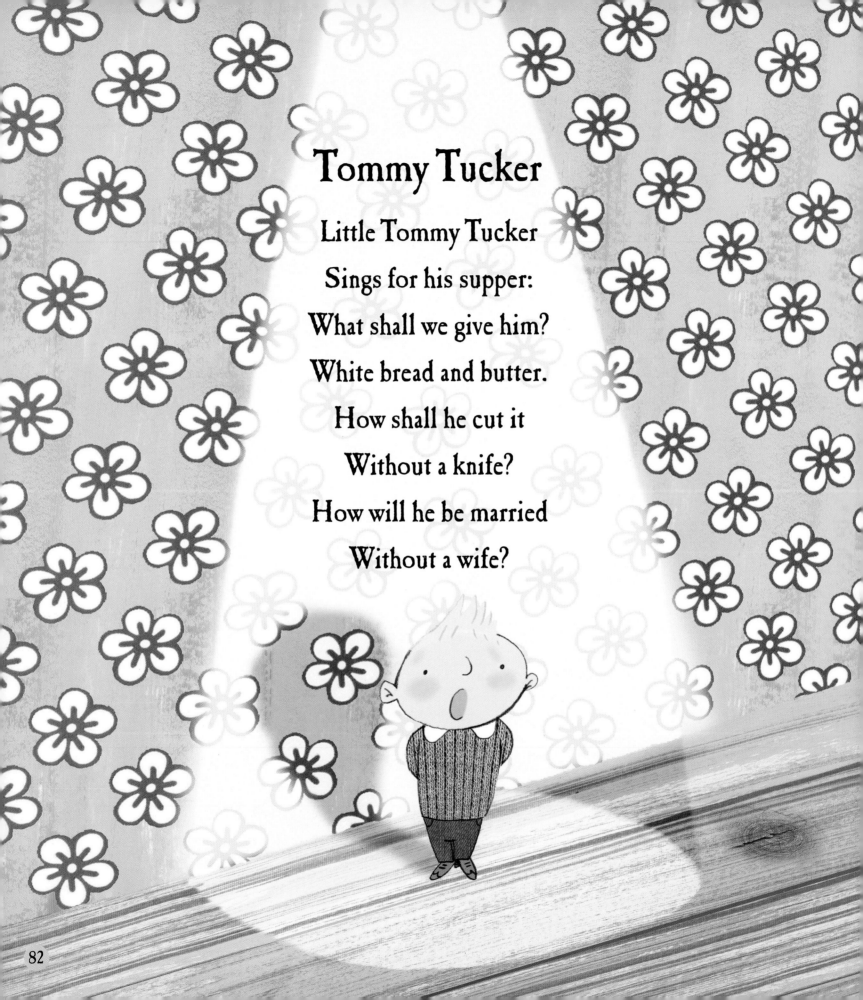

Old Mother Hubbard

Old Mother Hubbard went to the cupboard,

To fetch her poor dog a bone;

But when she got there, the cupboard was bare,

And so the poor dog had none.

Hush Little Baby

Wee Willie Winkie

Wee Willie Winkie runs through the town,

Upstairs and downstairs in his nightgown,

Tapping at the window, crying through the lock,

Are the children in their beds, for now it's eight o'clock?

Hush, Little Baby

Hush, little baby, don't say a word,

Papa's going to buy you a mocking bird.

If the mocking bird won't sing,

Papa's going to buy you a diamond ring.

If the diamond ring turns to brass,

Papa's going to buy you a looking glass.

If the looking glass gets broke,

Papa's going to buy you a billy goat.

If that billy goat runs away,

Papa's going to buy you another today.

89

Twinkle Twinkle, Little Star

Twinkle, twinkle, little star,

How I wonder what you are!

Up above the world so high,

Like a diamond in the sky;

Twinkle, twinkle, little star,

How I wonder what you are.

Star Light, Star Bright

Star light, star bright,

The first star I see tonight,

I wish I may, I wish I might,

Have the wish I wish tonight.

Rock-a-Bye, Baby

Rock-a-bye, baby, on the tree top,

When the wind blows the cradle will rock;

When the bough breaks the cradle will fall,

And down will come baby, cradle and all.

Bye, Baby Bunting

Bye, baby bunting,
Daddy's gone a-hunting,
Gone to get a rabbit skin
To wrap the baby bunting in.

I See the Moon

I see the moon, the moon sees me,

Under the shade of the old oak tree.

Please let the light that shines on me

Shine on the one I love.

Over the mountains, over the sea,

That's where my heart is longing to be.

Please let the light that shines on me

Shine on the one I love.

Index of Nursery Rhymes